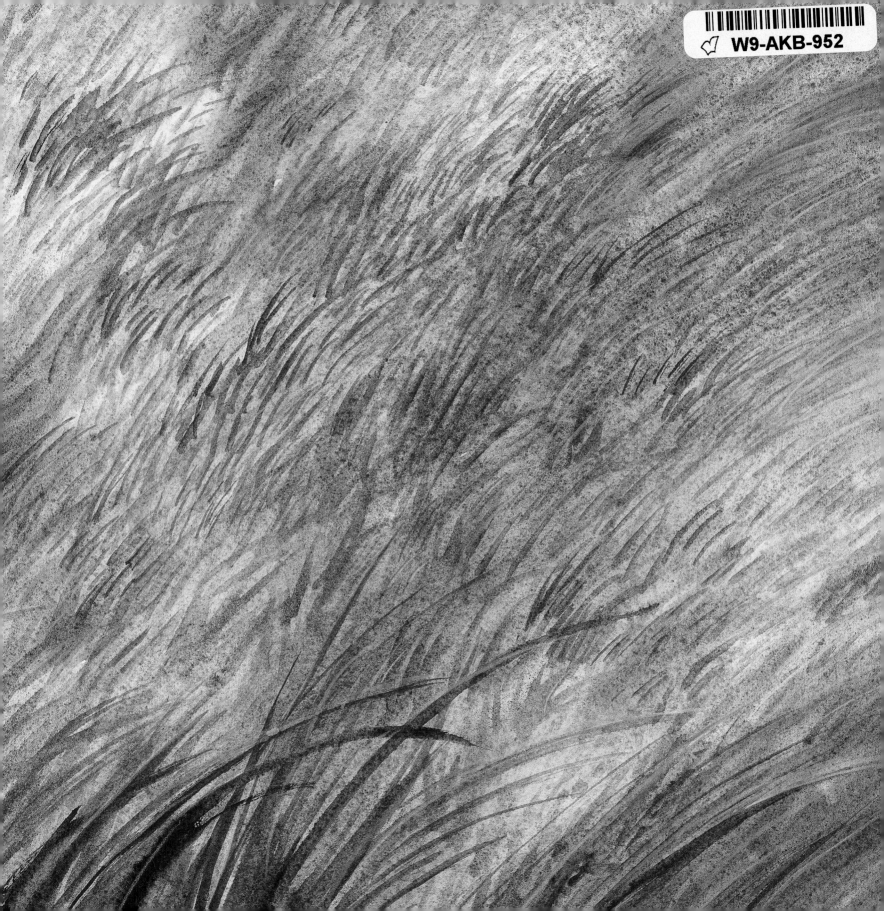

To Will and Dina
and
Always Friends everywhere

Copyright © 2021 by Jennifer Black Reinhardt
All rights reserved. Published in the United States by Random House Children's Books,
a division of Penguin Random House LLC, New York.
Random House and the colophon are registered trademarks of Penguin Random House LLC.

Visit us on the Web! rhcbooks.com
Educators and librarians, for a variety of teaching tools, visit us at RHTeachersLibrarians.com

Library of Congress Cataloging-in-Publication Data
Names: Reinhardt, Jennifer Black, author, illustrator.
Title: Always by my side / Jennifer Black Reinhardt.
Description: First edition. | New York : Random House Children's Books, [2021] | Audience: Ages 3–7. | Audience: Grades K–1. |
Summary: "A story showcasing the love between a child and their favorite toy" —Provided by publisher.
Identifiers: LCCN 2019050382 (print) | LCCN 2019050383 (ebook) |
ISBN 978-0-593-17382-4 (hardcover) | ISBN 978-0-593-17383-1 (library binding) | ISBN 978-0-593-17384-8 (ebook)
Subjects: CYAC: Toys—Fiction. | Friendship—Fiction.
Classification: LCC PZ7.R276 Al 2021 (print) | LCC PZ7.R276 (ebook) | DDC [E]—dc23

MANUFACTURED IN CHINA   10 9 8 7 6 5 4 3 2 1   First Edition

Always by My Side

A Stuffie Story

Jennifer
Black Reinhardt

Random House
New York

I will always
be by your side.

When you are cold,
I will keep you warm.

When you succeed,
I will jump for joy!

When you are sad,
I will hug you.

I will listen to your secrets
and never tell.

When you are afraid,
I will protect you.

And we will go on great
adventures together.

When you feel alone,
I will keep you company.

Together, we will learn new things.

We will create masterpieces

and explore new worlds.

We will build castles

and feel free.

I will watch you grow . . .

. . . and change.

We will always be together.
Even when we are apart . . .

. . . because I will always love you.

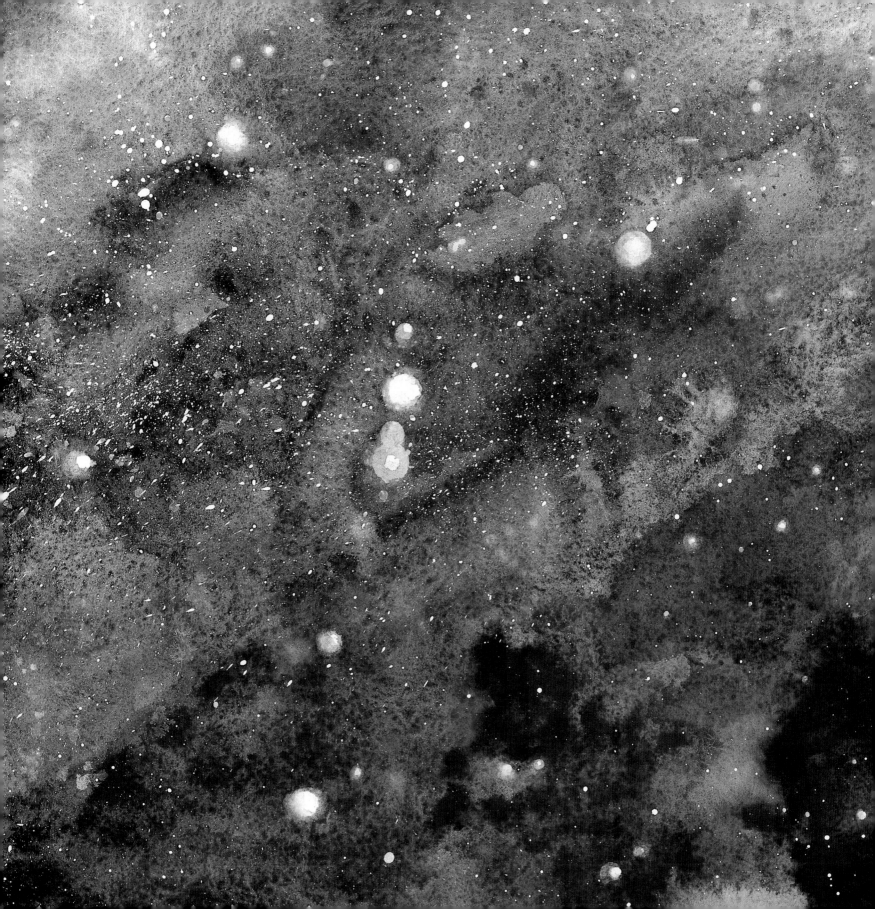

I will wait for you.

And be happy when you are home.

I will . . .

. . . always.